This Topsy and Tim
book belongs to

_____

Topsy + Tim

start school

Jean and Gareth Adamson

Ladybird

All Ladybird books are available at most bookshops, supermarkets
and newsagents, or can be ordered direct from:
Ladybird Postal Sales PO Box 133 Paignton TQ3 2YP England
Telephone: (+44) 01803 554761 *Fax:* (+44) 01803 663394
A catalogue record for this book is available from the British Library

Published by Ladybird Books Ltd
A subsidiary of the Penguin Group
A Pearson Company

© Jean and Gareth Adamson MCMXCV
This edition MCMXCVIII

The moral rights of the author/illustrator have been asserted
LADYBIRD and the device of a Ladybird are trademarks of Ladybird Books Ltd Loughborough Leicestershire UK

Topsy and Tim were off to school
after a fantastic summer holiday.
They felt happy and excited.
They walked straight past
their old playgroup.

Topsy and Tim were going to join
the bigger children at the Primary School.
They knew the Primary School was
a cheerful, friendly place.
They had been there already,
on a visit. But Topsy and Tim held hands
as they went through the big gateway.

'Oh, look,' said Tim.
'There's Tony Welch.'
'Hi, Tony!' called Topsy,
but her voice came out
not quite loud enough.

The Primary School was much noisier
than their old playgroup.
Some of the bigger children
did look very big.
Topsy and Tim soon met several
of their old friends, as well as Tony.

Miss Terry was
Topsy and Tim's
class teacher.

She showed them where to hang their coats and shoe bags. Each peg had a different picture by it.
'Remember your special picture,' said Miss Terry, 'and then you will know your own peg.'

'My peg's got a rabbit like Wiggles,' said Topsy. Tim's peg had a picture of a black umbrella.

He wasn't sure he could remember
an old umbrella.
'Girls always get the best things,'
grumbled Tim.

Mummy took Topsy and Tim
into their new classroom.
'There's Tony again,' said Topsy.
They went to see what he was doing.

Tony was busy doing a jigsaw puzzle.
'Would you like to do a jigsaw puzzle,
Topsy and Tim?' said Miss Terry.

Topsy and Tim found plenty of
interesting things to do.
There was sand to dig in and
water for sailing and sploshing.
The home corner had scales that worked.

When they felt like looking at books
and pictures, they sat on the carpet
in the quiet corner. The bell for
playtime seemed to ring too soon.

Miss Terry led the children into the school playground. It was full of big boys and girls all making a noise.

Topsy and Tim stayed close to Miss Terry
for a while.

Soon Topsy and Tim were playing happily
with some new friends. Then a big boy
rang a loud bell. Everybody stopped playing
and stood in lines to go back into school.

Dinner was served by two jolly ladies,
Mrs Knitting and
Mrs Pie. At least,
Topsy and Tim
thought those were
their names.
Topsy was
astonished to see
Tim eat all his
greens.

Afternoon school
was more like their
old playgroup.
Miss Terry
gathered all the
children round her.
They sang some
clever songs,
with actions.

When it was time to go home,
Topsy and Tim went to put on
their jackets.
'I can remember my peg picture,'
said Tim proudly. 'It's an umbrella.'
But Tim's peg was empty. Tim was upset.
'Never mind, Tim,' said Miss Terry.
'This often happens. I expect someone
knocked your things down and put them
back on the wrong peg by mistake.'

'Here's your jacket,'
called Andy Anderson.

'Did you enjoy your first day
at big school?' asked Mummy
on the way home.

'Of course we did!' said Topsy and Tim.